Whispered Wisdom

Books by Mary Summer Rain

Nonfiction

Spirit Song
Phoenix Rising
Dreamwalker
Phantoms Afoot
Earthway
Daybreak
Soul Sounds
Whispered Wisdom

Children's

Mountains, Meadows and Moonbeams

Whispered Wisdom

Portraits of Grandmother Earth

Mary Summer Rain

HamptonRoads
PUBLISHING COMPANY, INC.

   Hampton Roads Publishing Company, Inc.
   891 Norfolk Square
   Norfolk, VA 23502
   Or call: (804)459-2453
     (FAX: (804)455-8907

If you are unable to order this book from your local
bookseller, you may order directly from the publisher.
Call 1-800-766-8009, toll-free.

ISBN 1-878901-49-4

10 9 8 7 6 5 4 3 2 1

Printed in the United States of America

For Mumsie. . .

I know you can't get out here to Colorado so, as you look at each photograph in this book, I'd like you to imagine yourself standing beside me as I look through my camera lens to take the shot. Envision us together looking out at each scene. In this manner, mom, I will try to transport you to my beautiful Colorado and. . .to me. I love you, Mumsie. This one's for you.

Acknowledgements

To my beloved Grandmother Earth —
For the primeval Wisdom you have whispered from your sweet and
      gentle Breath. . .your timeless Wind,
For the warm Comfort you have radiated from your tender and
      sensitive Heart. . .your shimmering Core,
For the laughing Happiness you have sung from your coursing
      and eternal Life Force. . .your singing Streams,
For the deep Sensitivities you have instilled from your dignified
      and lustrous Spirit. . .your moonlit Mountains,
And for the Universal Truths you have revealed from your aged and
      ancient Bones. . .your Golden Canyons.
Each evening as my prayer smoke rises into the receiving night
      sky, I give thanks
        for the sharing
          of your ancient
            whispered wisdom.

Author's Foreword

As I walk through the serenity of a mountain woodland in the early morning hours when the misty remnants of wafting clouds still hang low and silent between the conifers, my mind is filled with the silver threads of meaningful thoughts.

When I stand within a wide valley amid the profusion of gently wavering wildflowers and breathe in the sweet essence of their colorful innocence, I think upon their offerings — their gifts.

While sitting in the depths of an autumn forest surrounded by the brilliant technicolor of nature in her final glory, I hear the soft rustling of the ruby and golden leaves, and I am filled with their gladness of life.

Standing beside a laughing mountain stream or perched atop a high country ridge where the wind circles and whispers, I listen to the wise voices of each and allow their wisdom to enter my being where there it is treasured and cherished.

Whether I hear the mountain's soft sighs, or whether my soul expands from the intense vastness of the sacred redstone mesas of the ancient canyonlands, makes no difference. Whether I hear the whispers on the wind, or whether I hear the cries of a People long gone from a barren and desolate land, makes no difference. I hear.

When I reach out to touch the entity of nature, she lovingly reaches back. She touches my mind and heart, soul and memory. And, because I am her child, because I love her, I hear her timeless words that are caught within the shimmering essence of her delicate spirit.

And to Grandmother Earth. . .I listen. . .I listen to her whispered wisdom.

The following represents a sampling of her whispered words that have inspired my own thoughts as I tread the mountain woodlands. It represents a loving sharing of what the mountains do breathe, what the streams do sing, what the wind does whisper. It represents the powerful Magic and Wisdom that rides the very breath of Grandmother Earth.

I give special thanks to Grandmother Earth for sharing her many Colorado faces within this book, and for her exquisite beauty, which has compensated for my amateur point-and-shoot photography style.

Autumn

*On the Sixth Day of Creation, God looked
over all He had made and saw that it was good.*

*On the Seventh Day, God surveyed the land
for a place to rest. . .*

and He called it Colorado.

Through Poverty I found Wealth.
Through Charity I found Happiness.
Through Acceptance I found Strength.
Through Patience I found Power.

Through Integrity I found Truth.
Through Sincerity I found Love.
Through Silence I found Voice.
Through Introspection I found Purpose.

Through Simplicity I found Peace.
Through Solitude I found The Knowing.
Through The Knowing I found The Great Alone.
Through The Great Alone I found The Within.
And. . .through The Within. . .I found God.

Looking in a mirror
And closing in nearer
I smile at what's there,
For my image is a mere
Face of some nonentity
Reflecting back at me.

It has been deemed
That I'm unseen,
But there's a choice
To hear the voice
Of one who imparts
What's in the heart.

And so no fame
Nor household name
Comes to me to be,
For in the end
The words we send
Are all there is to see.

So by and by
Don't look around
Nor drag thy
Heart upon the ground,
But harken to the wisdom found
Within the whispered sacred sounds.

The Hand of God reached far down and gently planted His precious seeds. Each beautiful seed had a special purpose. And within each seed was a gene of God's Will.

Some grew beautiful according to God's Will.
Some grew grotesque according to *their* will.

Autumn of Man came. It was Harvest Time. And God reached down and did gently harvest the beautiful blossoms. The weeds He did leave to reseed. In His compassion He gave the weeds another and another season to blossom according to His Will. Such was His love for each of His seeds.

Grow forth with your will abiding by His Will.
Grow forth toward the First Harvest.
Grow forth in Beauty.

Money, like honey, draws out the stinging bee.
Money, like honey, draws out the greedy bear.
Money, like honey, soothes the hungry palate and
smoothes into silk the coarse tongue.

Fairy wings and pixie dust
Crystal balls a must,
Magic runes and shaman cards
The New Age whole Nine Yards.

Sounds of shouted mumbo jumbo
From the mouth of ancient Rumbo,
"Hocus Pocus, look at me!"
Says the Master I. Have thee.

Mystic Potions, Sacred Lotions
Heal yourself with Hoodoo Motions,
Hear the Piper's flute and call
To little gods and goddess all.

Running here, chasing there
Like the racing tardy hare,
Seeking out the wizened faces
In remote and ancient places.

And false prophets
With full pockets
Woo the money
To the honey.

Bubble, bubble
Boils the trouble
Of the lot
Within the pot.

Smoke and Mirrors
Masked their fears,
And hid the cost
Of what they'd lost.

for. . .

They put their trust
In pixie dust,
And chose to follow
Down dark hollows.

all because. . .

The voice of their spirit —
They just couldn't hear it,
And so went ignored
The voice of the Lord.

Walk gently through life, for all the footfalls
must resound Respect.

Talk softly in life, for all the words must speak
Kindness.

Act prudently in life, for all the deeds must
manifest Peace.

Think compassionately in life, for all the thoughts
must echo Love.

In this Way do we live in a Sacred Manner.
In this Way do we reflect the soul of the Great
Mystery.

Did I hear you say,
The other day,
Autumn sings a sad song?
Oh no. . .you're wrong.
Autumn leaves may turn and fall,
But can't you hear its lifeforce call?
"All Endings are the Autumn leaves
That soon repose beneath white snows
Before they bloom as budding signs
Of Springtime's New Beginnings."

Strife comes from trying to fill the Void.
Peace comes from letting the Void fill Itself.

Snake Man basked upon a desert rock. Languidly did he turn this way and that until he smelled a new presence beneath the Saguaro.

Narrowing his beady eyes, he peered into the long shadow and spat forth his spray of words. "Turtle Man, so ugly and slow, leave me be, for I am most busy."

The One in cool shadow lifted his wrinkled neck to sway his head from side to side. "Busy? You are merely resting."

Snake Man closed his eyes in absolute disgust. "I am busy becoming beautiful!" He then sighed with the other's stupidity. "I will be famous for my beauty. Many will admire me. Go! All you ever do is struggle onward. You are slow. Leave me, stupid one!"

Turtle Man crept out from the cool shadow of rest and entered the blazing white heat. Onward he inched away from the pompous Snake Man. Onward he suffered and labored until a shadow passed over him. Turtle Man paused to crane his head up into the blinding sunrays.

Hawk Girl glided past the hot One on the baking desert floor. Her sympathy was great. Her sweet words were kind. "Have faith, Turtle Man, for your rewards will be great. Your heart is good and your suffering is long."

The slow One replied sorrowfully, "But I am not beautiful nor will I ever be admired like Snake Man."

Hawk Girl smiled and sang. "Ahh, but success is not judged by beauty or fame. It is judged by Efforts, Faith and Perseverance in *spite* of Long Suffering. Your determination is strong, Turtle Man, already you are a success. Already you are greatly admired by those who know the true value of your efforts."

This Moment in Time,
This One Footfall,
This Singular Breath,
This Heartbeat,
Is what some
        Choose to call
          A Lifetime.

Solemnly do I pray my Daybreak Benediction for the
world.
Respectfully do I hold my pipe and raise it in a sacred
manner.

North to the Wind Spirit, that It may blow fair.
West to Twilight, that all journeys may end well.
South to the Fire Keeper, that hearts won't grow
cold.
East to the Rising Sun, so It may light the Way.
Below to the Earth Mother, that She may be
healed.
Above to Wakan Tanka, that the Great Spirit may
hear.
Out to all Life Essence, that They may thrive.
And in to my Heart, where all Directions reside.

When I speak I am oft at a loss for words —
seemingly tongue-tied, dumb — for mortal language
has become so grossly inadequate for my thoughts.
How does one articulate the perspectives of the
Spirit when such concepts have no corresponding
words to speak them with?

Only through selfless Giving is the Spring Water freshened.

The Earth, its Moon, its Sun and neighboring Constellations are but a microcosm within the Totality of the Grand Design. Yet mortals, in their self-imposed Ignorance, still attain to discern and recognize delineating spatial boundaries that are nonexistent.

A Stranger, I,
Who walks through a strange land.
Never staying on delineating pathways,
But treads the Borderland Trails.

A Stranger, I,
Who casts two shadows,
One seen by all, One seen by none.

The Shadow Seen is real they claim
For it is of this world and time,
But the Shadow Unseen is just as real,
For it is of MY world and time.

And so I walk this Borderland,
Both Shadows very real,
One in front and one in back,
Connecting Spirit's Time.

Shadowland. Oh, Shadowland,
Softly do I tread thee,
For you give such peace and harmony,
To a Stranger such as I.

See you the mournful eyes of the Grief-stricken.
Peer into the hollow eyes of the Poor.
See you the sunken eyes of the Hungry, the Homeless.
Observe the glazed desolation of the Down-troddened.
Look!
See!
Then search within self!
For God does watch from behind the eyes of the many.

Knowledge is looking to the Horizon.
Wisdom is moving toward It.
Enlightenment is reaching It.
Illumination is journeying beyond It.
The Knowing is rising above It.

Exit Fear, for the very *existence* of fear does manifest that which one fears.

Freedom comes only after walking through the Door called Fear.

Some say that I'm an enigma. . .a mystery.
But where is it written that one must
parade before the public in order to
substantiate their validity of being?

Must the face be seen before the voice heard?
Must the body be touched before belief instilled?

Let not sight be your proof, for the eyes
do deceive.

Let not touch be your guide, for the physical
can be cloaked.

Instead, let the heart open wide to the validating
vibrations of the soul. . .only then is the mind an
accepted Vessel for The Knowing to fill.

There are some, many, spiritual beliefs that would appear as solid as stone, yet, when one approaches to examine them, they dissipate like a wavering mirage. . .merely droplets of mist.

And there are some, many, spiritual beliefs that would appear as abstract, as nebulous as a wavering mirage, yet when one approaches to examine them, they remain as solid as stone. . .an ancient, Eternal Stone.

I beheld a man who said, "Listen to me. I
will lead you, for I know all."
And lo, I beheld the King of Fools.

If all the pure Truths were picked up out of the present-day theological beliefs and spiritual philosophies, mortals would not yet hold the Totality of Truth, but merely behold a single Grain of Sand — a mere Atom of Truth's radiant Totality.

Hundreds thronged to the prophets' feet.
Crowds, eager and starry-eyed, were held
Entranced and hung on their every utterance.
Thousands came and more and more
To kneel, bow and give hypnotic homage.
In the Final Days. . .
This I did see.

One prophet was aged, or so it was believed
Wise beyond wise — all knowing.
His voice captivating and ringing so true
So that all in the great hall were
Mesmerized and convinced.
In the Final Days. . .
This I did hear.

And so it was, all these Last Days
When the prophets did call and the
Thousands did run toward the
Sound of the call.
Music to their ears was the
Pipers' sweet flute.
And so it would be I was told.
In the Final Days. . .
This I did know.

So I saw and heard and knew
As I watched and listened from afar.
While the sheep were flocking to the
Pretenders' voices, I waited for the
Final Hour when they'd see the wolfskins
And hear the hungry growls of the Beasts.
In tear-filled silence did I await the
Dawning of Truth. . .in silence did I hold
My lonely vigil where The Great Alone did
Shelter me from all the Chaos I saw and heard.

Let the scientists toil in their feeble attempts to dis-engage the Reasoning Mind from its Source.

Let the skeptics labor in their endless futile attempts to deny the Source within which the Reasoning Mind resides.

Let them toil and labor and deny — for the Spirit remains the undaunted Source, born of the Eternal Cause.

I heard the adulations as the
Excited hoards of people rushed
Past me.

Did I hear them murmur that the
Christ was over there?

Had my Advisors been wrong on
The foreseen timing?
Surely I would know if this was so.

I observed thousands flocking
About the gentle speaker.
More and more came running.

Standing far back I waited to
Spy the one who instilled such
Intense adoration and honor.

And when the crowd lowered
Themselves on bended knee,
My soul gave a jolting shudder.

For at that horrid moment did
I see the one standing tall
Above the crowd.

As he spoke his gentle words
My spirit did see his serpent tongue.
Did no one else see it?

With his arms upraised in holy
Blessing, my eyes did rest upon
The antichrist's disciple.

My Advisors had not been wrong.

And with a heart that felt as ice,
I slowly, very slowly. . .backed away.

As I mingle within the mass called Humanity, I gaze into the myriad faces. In the market, the shops, and along the many byways, I look into the smiling masks and wonder —

Where have all the *people* gone?

Winter

A seeker walked in deep despair, for he was greatly angered with his fate. He sat by the wayside and leaned against an old cottonwood. Looking about, he was blind to all he saw so great was his despair.

Outside the man's aura, nature sang songs of comfort to the lonely seeker. The wind gently whispered words of wisdom. The brook bubbled encouragement behind his back. Bees buzzed in colorful blossoms as they went about their labors. Above, birds soared and called. Sky, blue as blueberry pie, smiled down on him. High aloft, clouds drifted in meaningful shapes for him.

By and by, an insect passed the seeker's downcast vision. Toiling in the dirt, it went about its purpose until a swift hand swept it into oblivion and crushed its lifeforce.

And the seeker bemoaned his wretched fate. . .until he did spy a wise man coming his way.

He jumped to his feet and raced to the old one. "Are you the teacher I've been waiting for all these many years?"

The teacher, sad of eye and heavy of heart, replied softly, "No my friend, you've had many teachers already."

The seeker was shocked to hear this. "Sir, you're surely mistaken, have waited many years for my teacher to come."

"Yes," said the elder, "and in your high expectation have you closed your eyes and ears to your teachers. You have not listened to the greatest teacher of all — nature. In your expectation have you clothed your teachers in your own robes. In your expectation have you crushed your teachers and swept them from you."

The seeker cried, "But how could I have done this thing? How could I have crushed my teachers? You speak craziness, old man. You're no teacher. Move along! I await a great teacher!"

And so the great teacher did shuffle on past the seeker who returned to the cottonwood shade. . .to curse his fate. . .while crushing the pesky insects that crossed his vision by and by.

Spirit is of spirit.
Spirit is intangible.
Therefore do many still Thirst,
For they seek their quenching with tangibles.

The smallest pinpoints of celestial illumination
can only be seen within the darkest of nights.

And so it is with all things.

Fear not to walk forth within the Darkness — the
Unknown — for there alone does Illumination shine
brightest.

Spirit knows not a single paradox.

I saw a man who possessed great Power.
   The Power had no Color.
   The Power had no Name.
Should I fear or trust this man?
Then I looked within his heart.

In spellbound awe do I stand upon this lustrous ground of silvered moonlight. The hushed stillness of crystallite prisms fall gently over the mountain sentinels. I breathe deeply the incense of the crisp, rarified air. The snow, catching mirrored reflections of starshine, become minuscule rotating universes that gently tumble their brilliant constellations through infinity. And I silently upturn my palm to collect an entire shimmering cosmos that alights upon my hand. My soul does shudder with the enchanting moment I have witnessed. My heart does pound like a thousand drums, for on this sacred alpine night, I have seen and felt the raw, exposed soul of The One.

Oh, that I, such a meager specimen of humanity, could be allowed such joy within this transcendental surround, is truly evident of the Great Spirit's deep compassion and magnanimous unconditional love.

Universal Truths are not relative. Their deep conceptual existence is Absolute. Their Precepts are concrete Realities and can never be interpreted as possessing relative variances based upon differing perceptual levels of observation, pre-conceived theories or separate schools of thought.

Universal Truths are not relative.

Over a century ago, I saw the cordial meeting of two proud men. As they stood face to face — one washed and clothed in black robes, one painted and nearly naked — I could not distinguish which the missionary, who the pagan.

A man of great wealth did approach the wise one's door. He softly scratched on the worn wood to announce his arrival. He was given entry.

"Wise one," he began. "I've come with a great puzzlement that confounds my mind."

The seated man merely nodded for the stranger to speak his thoughts.

The wealthy man sat before the old one. "I have a dear friend, but I wonder about his soul. You see, my friend has lived a long life but he hasn't accomplished a single thing. His life has been for naught."

"For naught?" came the gentle reply.

"Why yes. What purpose was my friend's existence if he never accomplished anything?"

The old one closed his eyes then slowly opened them.

"Your friend, is he a kind man?"

"Yes, he is kind."

"This friend has a good heart then?"

The wealthy man chuckled. "Eh, too good. He works hard and then gives away most of what he earns. He's stupid."

"Stupid?"

"Yes, wise one, he gives away all his power. Because of this he never has the energy to accomplish anything."

The old one smiled. "Your friend's entire life has been an accomplishment. He *lives* it while you *choose* what to term an accomplishment. The more one gives of their power the more their vessel is refilled. Go my son, for now that you have been shown the true meaning of power, you will be held accountable for your use of it. Go now through life and make not accomplishments be events in your life, but rather make your entire life an event of accomplishment."

Ashamed, the stranger lowered his gaze and backed out of the wise one's simple abode.

I didn't come to be a teacher,
nor a leader be.
I didn't come to stand high before,
all to hear and see.
I didn't come for riches or fame,
nor to make prophetic claim.
I didn't come for gain of wealth,
nor even for myself.
I came because it was asked of me. . .
I came out of my love for Thee.

I wonder. . .
If all mortals gave more than they received,
If all mortals smiled more, offered more compassion
and frequent Kindness in Word and in Deed. . .
I wonder.

The State of Genius is but a fragmentary luminous Spark of the blinding Illumination contained within the Self.

Crystals possess great beauty.
Crystals possess great power.
So why so hard to see. . .to feel
That the greatest crystal is you?

I walk within a rich and verdant valley bounded by high mountain ranges.

The peaks to my right are called Predictable.

Those to my left are called Predetermined.

What separates the two is my valley. . .that is called Free Will.

Music   Number   Magic

The Grand Design Order is but the Music of the Spheres as orchestrated by the Master Composer at the Dawn of Creation.

The Universe

Eights upon Eights

Ordered Symmetry

Infinity

The celestial bodies dance to the Divine Symphony that plays the revealing ancient Formula. The musical Score that is heard is the Mathematical Key that unlocks the Ordered Symmetry of the Astronomical Unknown. And the Universe Enigma is no more.

Music   Numbers   Magic

Mephistopheles!
I call to you, Diablo.
Hear me?
I am one of the ones.
You know me, don't you.
Mephisto! Beware you Old Coyote!
Do you hear me?
I am one of the ones of The One.

"Who am I?" you ask.
Because I have come full circle,
Only now can I truly know and speak
of the who of me.

All the facets have been cut. . .the prism made whole.
What you see of the manifested me is but a mere
fragment of the real me.
So who am I?
I am no <u>one</u>. Now there can be no more me or I.
Now there is only. . .The Purpose. . .for that is all
that remains.

Death is not a state of mind.
Rather be it clarified as a Plane of Mind.
Yes. Death is a plane of mind.
Death is the transfer of the mind to a higher
energy vibration.
Therefore, in death do I continue to live on.
So. . .what then is death?
My mind lives on.
After death, I think.
Therefore, I am.
I am. . .always. . .
Mind Immortal.

THE LIGHT WARRIOR

Spirit's battles can come as a swift
Sword that plunges deeply.

Blood and tears flow.
They intermingle.
The defender is felled.

Raising blurred eyes to the Light,
The Spirit does know what must be done.

The Warrior grabs the hilt, extracts the blade
from self, and holds high the bloodied rapier.

The Warrior, struck down, transforms the painful
wound into a Sign of Strength — a Medal of Valor.

The Wound becomes the Mark of Power.
The Sword becomes the Coup Stick.
Together they become the Shield.

And the Warrior is empowered to fight on.

In the milling marketplace,
Within a crowded room,
Walking down the street,
Or driving through the town. . .
I feel The Great Alone.

Sitting on a mountaintop,
Resting by a stream,
Walking through a woodland green,
Or perched upon high buttes. . .
I feel The Great Alone.

But my heart does break,
And my soul does pain,
When I stand at night,
And scan the stars. . .
I ache The Great Alone
And pine for home.

There are times when one's great desire
for something causes the eventual attainment
to pale.

Desires, like high expectations, often prove
deflating. Therefore, the *power* of desire
must never outweigh the *value* of that which
is coveted.

Destiny knows not the clock nor the watch.
It knows not the reason for seasons and
sees no rhyme to manmade time.
Destiny unto itself is bound
to hear only its own metered sound.

Heavy is my heart this night,
It lies upon the ground.
For a Dark One came to laugh and boast,
How they'd won another round.

So my spirit has a bleeding wound,
My soul has falling tears.
But bright remains the living Light,
That banishes my fears.

Tonight I'll rest my weariness,
And heal the searing pains.
Come sun-up I'll be strong again,
To enter War's terrain

For the Dark and Light One's conflict,
Is a never-ending war.
Both sides fight hard and fierce,
'Til God says "Nevermore!"

Think upon this.

There are hundreds of splintered religions.

People use their Free Will to pick and to choose. One person chooses God's toe and calls it Religion. Another picks God's finger and declares it his Truth. Still another plucks a strand of God's hair and calls it Science. And they argue over whose portion of God is right.

They fight each other over it.

They disown each other over it.

They hate one another over it.

They even kill one another over it.

But their sight is myopic at best, for they do not see that God is God. And through their blinded infighting over truths they do not see how they are alienating themselves from the Heart of God.

His beautiful Wholeness, the shimmering DNA of His universal Totality, cannot be fragmented.

Take care who you strive to impress.
There is but one to please.

Care not what mortals would think of you, for their
minds are tainted by the self delusionary aspects of
false logic, poor judgement, egotism and skepticism.
Mortal minds are short-sighted and arrogant.

There is but one to please. . .
there is but one. . .
but one.
And the one is not self. . .
The One is God.

Spring

Time cannot be early or late,
    for Time knows not the terms.
Time has its own schedule based on
    the dictates of destiny.
Nothing can be early or late,
    for early and late <u>are</u> Time's chosen times.
Time cannot be hurried nor held,
    for Time is Destiny's mark of rightness.
Know that the right timing for things
    cannot be forced nor created by
    the simple efforts of mortal's desires,
    for Time is the master and bows to no one.
Time does not serve. . .it rules.

Oftentimes Truth is that which is most simplistic in concept — It is that which is clearly the obvious.

But mortals, with their penchant to complicate matters, clutters the purity of Truth and encumbers It until they can no longer recognize It.

My brother, how curious it is for me to see your rise to fame through everyone who suddenly knows everything about you. Volumes and volumes of books by the mortal "experts," by the many "channelers" by those who "know"; all write of you, your history your knowledge, your origins.

Everyone knows everything.

Yet when scanning these many simplistic volumes about you, it's so clear that nobody knows anything. How curious mortal nature is to devise so many illusions for personal fame's sake.

My Star Brother, I apologize for those everyones who know everything, for their eagerness at expertness has laid bare their ignorance. And, in their ignorance, have they become experts at nothing.

The Grand Helix of Life circles down from the Heavens, gathering together the core of each universe and the living life upon them. All that Is becomes intertwined.

The Grand Helix bonds, harmonizes and balances all of life as its transecting spirals continue their journey from forever into eternity—from the Source back into the Source.

After the Last there can be nothing else unless
it is its shadow or an imprint left behind.

> Last in line.
> Last of a kind.
> The End. Gone.
> Nevermore.

And so I stand alone now, for the Last of the
Line has gone. I wasn't even permitted a final
glimpse of the distancing shadow.
But when in sadness I bow my head, my eyes
discern the marks, for upon my trail, in clear
cast sand, are left her trailing footprints.

The Rainbow's graceful Arc, Lightning's jagged Streak,
The symmetrical Snowflake, shifting Canyon Shadows,
Autumn's golden Aspen, scarlet Alpenglow,
Flaming Fire in the western Sky —
All proclaim the Glory of
the Great Mystery.

Sacred Ways and Magic Days.
Things I've heard and Deeds observed.
Mystical Sights and Dream Soul Flights.
Cosmic Beings both large and small,
We've walked and talked so natural.
But pausing to ponder my proof of Truth,
my soul does sigh and heart does cry,
whilst mind asks why do men deny?

Before the fledgling can fly, it first must
leave the comfortable nest of security. Only
then does it rejoice in its exhilarating freedom.
Only then does it soar to new heights.

Nature. . .instinctual Wisdom.

The analytical mind is too often smothered by the judicious inspection of the fragmentary cells that obliterate the overall perception of the beautiful Totality of the Whole.

From the loins of the warmest emotion is born the coldest pain.

Love, the Giver and Destroyer both.

Love, the only Cup that pours forth the sweetest
nectar or bitterest brine — but only when it is full.

Love. . .alchemy of the heart.

I think too much.
My mind is ever steeped in thoughts
About the poor, the hungry children.
Visions of ragged homeless, cold and alone
Traipse their desolation before my mind's eye.
The sad song of Grandmother Earth plays
And replays through my mind, bringing
Pain with each remembered refrain.
The cries of the people, their misery; so
Many hurting and pleading with hope-filled
Eyes. So many voices. So many sad songs.
I think too much.
Or do I?

Scientific Method can only verify those
conceptual theorems confined within the
narrow limits of accepted physical laws.
Therefore does it fail to measure or even
perceive the spirit's capabilities — much
less validate its essential living essence.

The warty toad is not pretentious. It does not berate its Maker for its lack of beauty. It lives and thrives in spite of its outward affectations.

Perhaps it is far wiser than mortals who would strive to cloak that which they truly are.

I have been to a place where strangers are friends,
   Where Justice reigns,
   Where Truth is the Way.
I have been to a place where colors are vibrant,
   Where the music is sweet,
   Where sounds are harmonic.
How curious it is, how amazing the fact,
There's more life in Death than in Life.

Deep in white marble woods I heard through the trees
the sound of my name come beckoning to me. Its voice,
pure, like untouched crystal; its essence, clear, like fine
alpine air.

I turned around to follow the sound and deep in the
forest a wellspring I found. Its words were profound as
they flowed from the Source, and touched my soul to
reveal a new course. "I will stay here," I said, "for here I
belong." And Wellspring and I shared one soul song.

Then autumn came to claim my name and woodsmoke
drifted to hide my fame.

The wind sighed. . .
Leaves fluttered 'round. . .
Pinecones fell to ground. . .
Without sound.

Fear is oft the binding Root of Procrastination.

Entire lifetimes are spent in search of the Six Ultimates.
     Truth   Wisdom   Wealth   Happiness   Power   Love
Yet the more one strives, the more distant They become.
For the Ultimates reside within Simplicity,
And through Charity do they become manifest.

Each heartbeat is a gift from God.
And the Gift's name is Life.
Life is an extension of Time.

How then will you show your appreciation for
the next heartbeat given?

The Six Greatest Teachers have no face, no voice. . .
Yet Their students learn the most.

The Six Greatest Teachers are known by these names:

Long Suffering   Perseverance   Adversity
Acceptance   Tribulation   Charity

Where do I belong?
The White World feels so foreign. . .
and I feel so out of place.
The Native World feels so like home. . .
but all the doors are closed.

Whites don't like my native heart,
Natives say I need the papers.
Some folks call me misfit,
Others think me crazy.

I look around and pine to find. . .
a place where I belong.
I look around and try to spy. . .
a face of my own kind.
But after many years it's clear,
I've only found it in the mirror.

The word of welcome, when I hear it,
Comes only from my spirit.
There the sweetest songs I hear,
Sing words that draw a tear,
For I was meant to walk alone,
Where no path leads to home.

And so that's how it is to be,
These hours that I live for Thee.
So I will bear this Shadowland,
Until once more You take my hand,
To grant me rest and make me whole,
Back Home again within Your Soul.

They came for one of us again.
They came in stealth and in disguise.
I saw the bent shadow of the Old Crone.
Turning, she glared right at me.
A grim smile twisted her wicked lips.
Our eyes locked in battle for a precious life.
Her smile faded then,
And the dark specter turned to leave empty-handed.
I glowered at the retreating figure.
"Not today, Old Crone. You cannot take my Sarah
with you today."
And I sighed a long and weary breath,
"No, you cannot rip out my heart. . .not today."

Knowledge and Charity are as the right and the
left ventricle of the Visionary's heart.

Round out your thinking,
For all things Above and Below are interconnected.
We are major components in the Great Hoop of Life,
Circling, always circling.
Arch the linear.
Curve the corners.
Bend the angles.
Arc the points.
Round out your thinking,
For life is not dead ends.
Life is not being cornered.
Nor is it being up against a wall.
Life is a flow of continuum. . .
One phase gently flowing along the Hoop. . .
One arcing into the other.

The Universal Truths are immutable.
They cannot be fragmented by ceremonies.
They do not demand ritual.
Yet I see many rites performed in their Name.

The Universal Truths are the Essence of Purity.
They cannot be tagged by sects.
They do not demand dogma.
Yet I see many belief systems formed in their Name.

The Universal Truths are The Universal Truths.
They cannot be termed otherwise.
They do not equate to men's various translations.
Yet I hear many strange words uttered in their Name.

The Universal Truths are not the rituals.
They are not the belief systems.
They are not even the words.
Oh no, they are not the words. . .
They are the Breath.

A visionary spoke in a crowded marketplace where rich and poor alike did gather shoulder to shoulder. Silence settled over the mass of listeners as the wise one softly spoke.

When the talk concluded, one man turned to his neighbor and shrugged. "Eh, he must not value his wisdom much to be giving it away like that. I usually go pay to hear the really good ones. Now that's where you really get your money's worth!"

The man's neighbor smiled warmly, for he had no words of wisdom to retort with. He was too filled with the powerful words of enlightenment that the visionary had touched his heart with.

So tell me, which man knew the true value of wisdom?

The one who judged it by how much money he had to put out for it or the one who judged it by what he gained and how he was touched within?

Which knew the high wisdom of spiritual value?

Summer

Your sunny day is my starry night
. . .yet we share the same shining sun.
Your warm summer is my snowy winter
. . .yet we share the very same date.
Your desert home is my mountain home
. . .yet we share the same rushing river.
Your tropic jungle is my piney forest
. . .yet we share the same air and rain.
So far apart do we live
. . .yet so much do we share.
What you do affects me, what I do affects you.
Your home is not over there, mine not over here.
Yours is mine, mine is yours.
Ours is Earth. . .a Blanket Shared.

Those who strive to create their own reality are in a constant state of struggle and strife for self-satisfaction and attainment of personal goals. They cannot help but fight against the stream's Current of Life as they reject that which has been meant to lie upon their paths.

Such struggling ones are not at rest and cannot obtain the State of Acceptance and Peace that is essential to the ultimate Oneness with All That Is.

Therefore is their Within State cluttered and muddied by the aggravations and din of the Without State Chaos.

I wish I could speak of That Which Dwells within my mind,
    but my tongue cannot say the words,
    for there is no one word to give It meaning.

I wish I could express That Which Dwells within my heart,
    but my actions cannot externalize the feelings,
    for there is no one emotion to give It a name.

I wish I could share That Which Dwells within my spirit,
    but my words and actions are too inadequate,
    for there is no one mold to give It form.

    Wordless.   Nameless.   Formless.

Therefore do I keep the Great Mystery that dwells within me a sacred Thing — ever cherished, protected and loved.

The greatest effects are caused by the simplest means.
Simplicity. . .the Key that unlocks many doors.

Cling not to the Spiritual Teacher,
For teachers do pass from your world.
Cling to the teacher's words,
For Truth cannot be killed.

Shhh. Be still. Listen.
Something wonderful this way comes.
Shhh. Can you hear it? Feel it?
The New World is but a heartbeat away.

Shhh. Listen harder.
Someone glorious this way comes.
Shhh. Can you hear the footfalls approaching?
The presence of The One is but a whisper away!

If you care not for Today and
Your Yesterdays hold no
spiritual Word or deed, what
are you doing here?

What are you doing?

Have a care. Have a care.
For Tonight may
quickly wane into
Your last Tomorrow.

A noble deed is a deed
that precludes reward.

In the depths of my quietude, while sitting upon a mountain boulder, there is a metered vibration felt, for nature hums beneath her breath. In a myriad of harmonizing pitches and tones does nature forever sing her Song of Life. And my ear does attune to the celestial melody of the living Singing Stones.

Coincidence is the mark of Destiny.

My soul makes weeping sounds
To see so many mortals
Claiming to be God.

My heart sheds bleeding tears
To see so many mortals
Claiming to be Christ.

It was foretold when God
Returns, the world will
Shudder at the sight.

For Light and Glory will
Surround His legions of
Angels ready for battle.

And it was foretold before
His coming, that many would
Claim His face and name.

For the Dark Ones will delight
and revel, in donning the Robes
of His Light.

And because this last has
Come to be. . .
My soul makes weeping sounds
And my heart sheds bleeding tears.

When life is lived for dreamed-of Tomorrows
All the Todays are but grey Shadows
That make one's Yesterdays unremarkable.

The Waves of Time Alone are illusionary.
The Waves of Time Alone are stationary.
Look you to the energy of the *Current*,
For its *velocity* is the Corridor of Space *and* Time.

Everything is Nothing.
Thriving is the Void.
Crowded is the Emptiness.
And The Nothing is the
Womb of Everything where
The All undulates within
The One.

In another time,
And in another place,
The Anasazi had
Another name and face
. . .the Essenes.

In another time,
And in another place,
The Essenes had
Another name and face
. . .the Starborn.

The anxious novice inquired of the wise sage, "Tell me Wise One, what does a mystic experience feel like?"

In sweet remembrance, the visionary smiled. "Wonderful."

"Wonderful? But that's such a common word," frowned the disappointed student.

"Yes, so it is."

"Well, what do you *see* in your mystical journeys?"

"Beauty," came the simple reply.

Unsatisfied, the student remained puzzled. "But how does it all work? How does one sustain a mystical journey?"

"By non-thought," the sage responded.

"Where do you *really* go when you journey?"

"Into the Emptiness that is Full."

"But how can an emptiness be full?"

The teacher smiled warmly. "I cannot tell you that."

"Why can't you tell me this?"

"Because there are no words to say it with."

Again the young one frowned. "No words, sir?"

The sage's palms upturned then. "My little friend, you ask me to describe feelings, sights, pathways and places that are of the highest dimensions, but then you encapsulate my language within the confines of the simple third dimension. What you ask cannot be answered by choosing words out of a child's primer. What you seek is not a statement. . .what you seek is called *The Knowing*."

The novice thought hard on that. Finally he concluded, "Then I will go and *seek* The Knowing."

The visionary merely shook his head. "No my little friend, you do not go to *It*. . .The Knowing comes to *you*."

Our vast solar system
Is but the nucleus
Within one atom
Of the living Body
Of the Void.
For we are within The All,
And so The All is within us also.
Everything is every thing.
There is no Ones,
Except the Pattern of The All.

Knowledge alters Perspective.
Wisdom alters Thought.
Enlightenment alters Value.
Illumination alters Life.
And. . .The Knowing alters All.

My troubles, so many.
My pains, so deep.
My battles, so fierce.
My enemy, so strong.
So ignorant, the foolish,
So ripe they become.
So joyous the Dark Sons,
So victorious they become.
*For those who **disbelieve** in the Dark Ones,*
They become such easy prey.
*For those who **know** of the Dark Ones,*
They suffer the wounds of war.
Troubles. Pains.
Losses.   Scars.
Yet I am here and still endure,
For the Sons of Light shall overcome,
And their wounds shall set them free.

When one strives to manifest self according to the standards and mores consistent with others' many expectations. . .that one will gaze upon his own mirrored reflection, yet never will he see himself.

Breathing in the Smoke

Smudge smoke
　　　of cedar and sage.
Incense smoke
　　　of frankincense.
And. . .
Smoke of my pipe
　　　infuses my being.
Smoke of my pipe
　　　rises to the sky
Smoke of my pipe
　　　carries my prayers
　　　　upon its sacred breath.

When I painted my face and charged. . .none took notice,
for they thought me a harmless fool.

And when I walked in peace. . .they attacked, for they thought me a dangerous threat.

STILL FRIENDS

We had a falling out
The Starman and I,
For I couldn't understand
Why we couldn't proceed.

I paced before him,
And stomped my foot.
With logic I questioned,
With reason I argued.

So calm he was,
With voice so soft.
He listened well,
To all I said.

But the visit ended
As many did,
With a solid impasse
With no resolution.

"Timing," he insisted,
"Is too important,"
And whispered, "Our Time
Has not yet come."

So there were those nights
When I'd wait 'til dawn
For him to come
And visit again.

I had to try
To plead my case —
To speed The Plan,
To give our proof.

But I'd wait in vain,
For he knew the words
I'd say were just
A force on Time.

We have falling outs
The Starman and I,
But still we know
We live as friends.

No-Eyes knew
As Many Heart knew
That Starman knows
The heart of me.

Turning their heads, closing their eyes and covering their ears, they jeered at the warning message.

For, they laughed, the messenger was a clown.

So when warning bells rang and sirens did scream, they turned their heads with eyes held wide to seek the one they called the clown.

But clown couldn't be found.

Clown wasn't around.

Clown was gone.

And so concludes a sampling taken from the "tattered notebook" that serves as my woodswalking companion. No-Eyes' wish to see my thoughts shared has now been manifested. In this manner do I lovingly honor her.

So has it been requested.
So has it been written.
Now my heart is full.

Books by Mary Summer Rain

Since 1985, when *Spirit Song* first appeared, un-counted thousands have discovered Mary Summer Rain and "No-Eyes," the wise old Native American woman who taught the young Mary Summer Rain many things.

Spirit Song: The Visionary Wisdom of No-Eyes (1985), told how the two first met. Although totally blind from birth, No-Eyes lived on the land, identifying everything she needed by smell and touch. Using gentle discipline, humor, and insight, she guided Summer Rain through a remarkable series of experiences, giving her the accumu-lated knowledge of her own eight decades.

Phoenix Rising: No-Eyes' Vision of the Changes to Come (1987), used the analogy of the phoenix, the mythical bird that symbolizes rebirth and eternal life, to provide a powerful warning of the earth changes in store for us. This unforgettable prophecy has already begun to come true, as the daily newspaper and TV news broadcasts demonstrate.

Dreamwalker: The Path of Sacred Power (1988), told how No-Eyes introduced Mary to Brian Many Heart, who taught Mary the power of the Dreamwalker by bringing her to face many painful realities.

Phantoms Afoot: Journeys Into the Night (1989), is a fas-cinating description of the quiet work done by Mary and her husband Bill in liberating spirits lost between two worlds. You might call these ghost stories, but ghost stories told with concern for the welfare of the ghost! Like the previous three volumes, *Phantoms Afoot* is very much set in Colorado. All the wild beauty of the Colorado countryside enters into the story.

Earthway (1990), Mary Summer Rain's fifth book, is a presentation of the knowledge of the Native Americans.

Interweaving the inspired teachings of No-Eyes with a wealth of practical knowledge of all kinds, she demonstrated a practical, gentle, *civilized* way of life. Divided into sections for body, mind and spirit, the book aimed at restoring wholeness.

Daybreak: The Dawning Ember (1991), Mary's sixth book, is divided into two parts. "The Communion" consisted of extensive answers to questions she had received from readers over the years. Ranging from prophecy to Native American history, from metaphysics to just plain common sense, here were nearly 450 pages of wisdom, including an extensive section on dream interpretation.

The second section, called "The Phoenix Files," is a comprehensive collection of maps, charts, lists, and tables describing nuclear facilities, toxic-waste dumps, oil refineries, hurricane, tornado and flood-hazard zones, as well as a suggested pole-shift realignment configuration. Together, it made an indispensable resource manual.

Soul Sounds: Mourning the Tears of Truth, is the book Mary's readers long waited for: her own story, in her own words, of the experiences that shaped her extraordinary life, from childhood to her most recent meetings with Starborn friends. This was her private journal, written for herself and for her children. She didn't want it published. But her advisors insisted, and finally she gave in. . . .and the reader reaction has been nothing shor of phenomenal.

Mountains, Meadows and Moonbeams: A Child's Spiritual Reader (1984, 1992), was originally privately printed by Mary and Bill. Only in 1992 was the first trade paperback edition made available by Hampton Roads Publishing Company. This simple, delightful, easy-to-read book is full of illustrations for coloring; it will help parents nurture the creativity and imagination of their children; and will help children to understand where we come from and who we as humans really are.

HAMPTON ROADS
PUBLISHING COMPANY, INC.

Books for the body...
    health, beauty, nutrition...
Books for the mind...
    fiction, history, psychology, parapsychology,
    current events, regional...
Books for the spirit...
    spiritual, inspirational, practical, "new age"...

Would you like to be notified as we publish new books in your area of interest? Would you like a copy of our latest catalog? Fill in this page (or copy it, if you would prefer to leave this book uncut), and send to:

Hampton Roads Publishing Co., Inc.
891 Norfolk Square
Norfolk, VA 23502

[___] Please send latest catalog

[___] Please add me to the following mailing list(s):

    [___] Books for the body

    [___] Books for the mind

    [___] Books for the spirit

NAME_____

ADDRESS _____

CITY _____STATE_____ ZIP _____